MAY 2018

Lulu
My Glamorous Life

READ ALL THE
LOTUS LANE BOOKS!

LOTUS LANE

Lulu

My Glamorous Life

by Kyla May

BRANCHES

SCHOLASTIC INC.

As they say, there's no "i" in "team."
To Claire, Lisa, and Paul, my fabulously talented team.
Thanks for helping me see my imaginary worlds.

No part of this publication may be reproduced, stored in a retrieval system, or transmitted in
any form or by any means, electronic, mechanical, photocopying, recording, or otherwise, without
written permission of the publisher. For information regarding permission, write to Scholastic Inc.,
Attention: Permissions Department, 557 Broadway, New York, NY 10012.

Library of Congress Cataloging-in-Publication Data
May, Kyla. Lulu : my glamorous life / by Kyla May.
p. cm. — (Lotus Lane ; 3)
Summary: Lulu, one of the Lotus Lane Girls, loves all things sparkly and glamorous,
so when she hears about a Penelope Glitter look-alike contest she is determined to enter
and win—and she is not going to let the still-unresolved problems with neighbor Mika get in the way.
ISBN 978-0-545-44516-0 — ISBN 978-0-545-49618-6 — ISBN978-0-545-49682-7
1. Lookalikes—Juvenile fiction. 2. Contests—Juvenile fiction. 3. Best friends—Juvenile fiction.
4. Neighbors—Juvenile fiction. 5. Diaries—Juvenile fiction. [1. Lookalikes—Fiction. 2. Contests—Fiction.
3. Best friends—Fiction. 4. Friendship—Fiction. 5. Neighbors—Fiction. 6. Diaries—Fiction.]
I. Title. II. Title: My glamorous life.
PZ7.M4535Lul 2013
813.6—dc23

ISBN 978-0-545-49618-6 (hardcover) / ISBN 978-0-545-44516-0 (paperback)

14 13 12 11   17 18 19 20/0

Printed in the USA   23
First Scholastic printing, September 2013

TABLE OF CONTENTS

THIS DIARY BELONGS TO

Lulu

Chapter 1

Surprise!?!

Tuesday

Dear Diary,
It feels so great to finally write those words!
I'm going to do it again:

DEAR DIARY . . .
I've wanted one of you
ever since my friends Kiki
and Coco got diaries. Then,
this morning at school, I
opened my locker, and there
you were, all wrapped up in
a pretty bow!

Kiki and Coco saved up and bought you for me as a present. Now everyone in the LLGC has a diary!

What's the LLGC?
It's the Lotus
Lane Girls Club.
Lotus Lane is the
prettiest street
in Amber Acres.
It's where all the
LLGC girls live.

Who are the LLGC girls? They are me,
Lulu Lissette Lyons . . .

me

Bosco is my cat who thinks she's a dog

my **BFF** Kiki, the fashion star . . .

Kiki

. . . Maxi

and my other BFF Coco, the baker.

Coco

Lucky

Evie

This is our club's weekly calendar of activities. As you can see, we're a busy bunch.

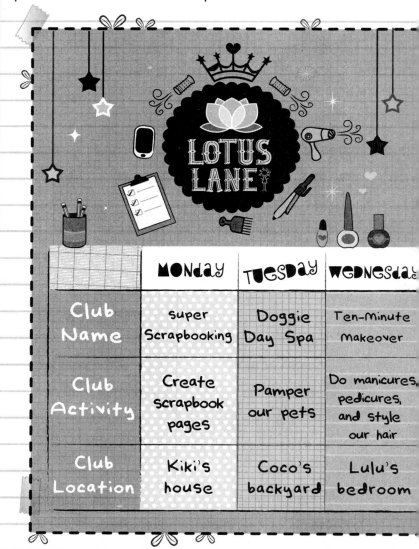

	MONDAY	TUESDAY	WEDNESDAY
Club Name	super Scrapbooking	Doggie Day Spa	Ten-Minute Makeover
Club Activity	Create scrapbook pages	Pamper our pets	Do manicures, pedicures, and style our hair
Club Location	Kiki's house	Coco's backyard	Lulu's bedroom

LOTUS LANE Girls Club schedule

THURSDAY	FRIDAY	SATURDAY	SUNDAY
LOTUS DAY OFF	Pajama Party	Cupcake Catch-Up	LOTUS DAY OFF
	Watch movies, eat popcorn, gossip	Bake cupcakes	
	Kiki's, Lulu's, or Coco's house	Coco's kitchen	

5

Besides my BFFs, the other big people in my life are my family. My dad is French — as in, from France. He writes books. So does my mom. The books they write are called <u>self-help</u> books. These books help people help themselves . . . which is helpful.

Dad

YES YOU CAN

YOU ARE YOU

Mom

I also have an older sister named Chantal, who's in high school. Chantal is super cool! All of the LLGC members want to be just like her some day.

Chantal

A VERY important thing you need to know about me is that I love making lists. Here is a list of the kinds of lists I like to make, or, as I like to call it, a <u>list list</u>.

My LIST LIST

- Daily To-Do Lists
- Emergency Lists
- Homework Lists
- Packing Lists
- Birthday Present Lists
- Books-to-Read Lists
- Shopping Lists (my favorite!)

You can make lists about everything. They are very helpful and can help you (me!) think better.

Okay, well, I have to do homework and get some sleep. But don't worry, Diary, I'll tell you more tomorrow!

Chapter 2

It Girl!

Wednesday

To Do
- Go to school
- Go to **TMM**
- Tell Diary more about ME!

TMM = Ten-Minute Makeover

Okay, Diary . . . where was I?

Well, besides making lists,
I also LOVE giving makeovers!
I like helping people look great with hairstyles,
makeup, fashion . . . that kind of thing.

Check out this great
new hairdo I gave Kiki
at TMM today!

KIKI

And look at how
I did Coco's hair!

COCO

Another BIG thing I love: Penelope Glitter! She's
the star of the Sleuth Sally movies, which I (and
my BFFs) LOVE LOVE LOVE. Penelope and I like
a lot of the same things. . . .

PENELOPE LIKES

- Looking **glamorous**
- Makeovers
- Award shows
- Red carpet events
- Fashion magazines

GLAMOROUS = looking all dressed up and totally gorgeous

RED CARPET EVENT = a fancy event that famous people attend

LULU LIKES

- Looking glamorous
- Makeovers
- Award shows
  (I once came in second place in the school spelling bee!)
- Red carpet events
  (Okay, I've never actually been to one, but my mom's red satin bathrobe makes a great red carpet.)
- Fashion magazines

11

Ooh . . . Lookie here . . . I read fashion magazines to get makeover ideas and today must be my lucky day. . . . Penelope Glitter is on the cover of *It Girl!* magazine! This must've come in the mail last week — how did I miss it?! I can't wait to see what's inside!

Diary — You're not going to believe this!

It Girl! is holding a Sleuth Sally Look-Alike Contest. In each Sleuth Sally movie, Penelope Glitter dresses up as a different secret spy to solve the latest mystery. All I have to do for the first round of the contest is text in a photo of me dressed like a Sleuth Sally spy character. There are three rounds to get through. But then the winner gets to go to a Sleuth Sally movie **premiere** and meet Penelope Glitter!

PREMIERE = first time something is being seen

But wait — there's more: The winner also gets to walk the red carpet and take a picture with Penelope Glitter. And the photo will be printed in *It Girl!*

You know what that means? I could meet Penelope Glitter!

But it says I have to enter the contest by Friday — that's just two days away! <u>EEK</u>! Calling Kiki and Coco right now!!!

"Should I enter the contest?" — me

"She's not seriously asking that question, is she?" — Kiki

"Nah, she can't be." — Coco

"No one knows more about Sleuth Sally! ENTER THE CONTEST!!!" — Kiki and Coco

They're right. I do know everything there is to know about Sleuth Sally, from the way she walks to how she flicks her hair. It's like a test I've been studying for half my life. All I have to do is dress up like a Sleuth Sally spy character, take a photo, and send it in. Which is something I do all the time anyway. (Well, without the sending-in part.)

#1

And if I win, I get to meet my number-one **idol**, PENELOPE GLITTER!!!

IDOL = someone you really like or look up to

I'm so excited! But I have to sleep. I hope you enjoyed our second day together! I know I did. Good night!

~~~~~~~~~~~~~~~~~~~~~~~~~~~~~~~~~

Diary, is it tomorrow yet?

I just looked at the clock. It is very NOT tomorrow yet. But I can't sleep. I keep putting together different Sleuth Sally looks in my mind. Too bad she never dressed up like Mr. Sandman . . .

The good news: I've decided I'm going to dress like Sleuth Sally as Rock 'n' Roll Rachel! Rachel's so cool, and she rocks awesome platform boots. See?

platform boots →

The bad news: I still can't fall aslee—

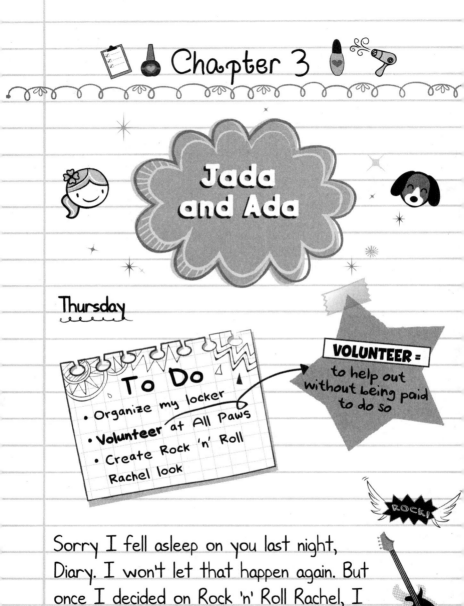

Chapter 3

Jada and Ada

Thursday

To Do
- Organize my locker
- **Volunteer** at All Paws
- Create Rock 'n' Roll Rachel look

VOLUNTEER = to help out without being paid to do so

ROCK!

Sorry I fell asleep on you last night, Diary. I won't let that happen again. But once I decided on Rock 'n' Roll Rachel, I did feel so much better.

After school today I'm going to volunteer at All Paws. It's an animal **shelter** where pets go to be adopted. I go there every week with Chantal. It's our special thing that we do together.

SHELTER = a place that houses lost animals

Chantal's class visited All Paws once. Chantal liked it so much that she kept going back to help out. She thought I would like it, too, because I ♥ dogs. And she was right. I love going there with her! I help **groom** the animals, just like I do in Doggie Day Spa.

GROOM = to clean, brush, shine, cut, shape . . .

I'm off to school now. I'll write again after All Paws!

Today, a girl named Jada came in with her parents. She looked about my age, and she seemed sad. When I asked her what was wrong, she said, "My beagle died last month." She showed me his picture. He was so cute!

JADA

her beagle

"I'm so sorry," I said to her. But then I remembered something. "Hey, All Paws is getting in a beagle next week. She's a rescue dog. Do you want us to save her for you?" I asked.

Jada's face lit up. "Could you?"

I told Jada to come back next Thursday. I took Jada's photo because she looked so happy. Then I ran to tell Chantal so that she could talk to Jada's parents about the dog.

Then I remembered something else so I ran back over to Jada.

"The beagle's name is Ada!" – me

"That rhymes with Jada! Oh, I can't wait to meet her!" – Jada

I didn't think of the contest the whole time I was at All Paws. WOW. Helping others can really take your mind off of yourself . . . you know? Okay, Diary, I have to think more about my look for Rock 'n' Roll Rachel. Then time to sleep . . .

Chapter 4

In the Bag

Friday

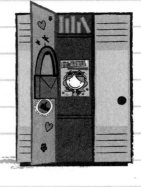

To Do
- Create Rock 'n' Roll Rachel look
- Show L L G C
- Text pic to contest!!!
- Hang new <u>It Girl!</u> cover in locker
- Prep for sleepover

Rise and shine, Diary! I woke up SUPER early today to dress up like Rock 'n' Roll Rachel and send in my pic before school.

Lulu: Here I am as Rock 'n' Roll Rachel:

Kiki: Those boots look awesome!

Coco: Rachel rocks!

Rachel's getting a lot of love. Good thing because I just sent that photo into the contest . . . EEK! Okay, I have to change and get to school! TTYL!

TTYL = talk to you later

I have to tell you what happened at school today. But first, here's . . .

The Story of
Katy Krupski

KATY KRUPSKI

Once upon a time, there was a Katy Krupski. She was very mean, and her meanness began all the way back in kindergarten. That's when she put craft glue in my hair, and my mom had to cut it out. It was an ending (of my long hair) but also a beginning (of my then short hair). That also might have been the beginning of my love for hairdos and hairstyling.

So <u>today</u>, when I was minding my own business, hanging up the new magazine cover in my locker, Katy Krupski walked by and said:

"Lulu, I know you like Penelope Glitter, but don't bother with the *It Girl!* contest. I've so got it in the bag!" – **Katy**

(What bag??? I guess that means she thinks she'll win. What a show-off!!!!)

IN THE BAG

I'm not going to listen to Katy. But why does she have to be so mean?

Kiki and Coco are about to come over for tonight's Pajama Party. Also in the house tonight – Mika. Mika is our new neighbor. Kiki and Coco invited her since she was so helpful with Coco's Cupcake Sale last week (the one that raised money for the school vegetable garden).

CUPCAKE SALE

I still haven't decided what I think of Mika. She was helpful last week, but I'm not sure I trust her because she's really good friends with Katy! I wish I was as clever as Sleuth Sally — then I'd know for sure if I could trust Mika.

I think this calls for a list. . . .

TRAIT =
a quality a
person has

MIKA

FRIEND TRAITS:

Helpful:
Baked cupcakes for cupcake sale

Caring:
Kept the money from the cupcake sale safe

Likes the Same Things as me:
Sleuth Sally

ENEMY TRAITS:

Friends with the Enemy:
Katy Krupski

Whether Mika's a friend or not, I'm excited about tonight's Pajama Party because Kiki and Coco are true friends, through and through. They're giving Mika a chance — so I will, too!

Chapter 5

Friend or Foe?

Saturday

> **FOE =** enemy

To Do
- Admit I was wrong
- Think about the contest
- Cupcake Catch-Up

Okay! I admit it. I was wrong about Mika. We all had fun together at the sleepover last night.

So . . .

MIKA

FRIEND TRAITS:

TAKE 2

Helpful:
Suggested looks and hairstyles for if I make it to round #2

Fun:
Showed us cool dance moves from her hip-hop class

Good Snack Bringer:
Brought Japanese treats, like green tea ice cream. Mmm, mmm, good!

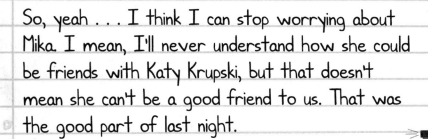

So, yeah . . . I think I can stop worrying about Mika. I mean, I'll never understand how she could be friends with Katy Krupski, but that doesn't mean she can't be a good friend to us. That was the good part of last night.

But, Diary, there was also a bad part of last night, and, boy, was it bad. Very bad.

Here's what happened:

> "I brought a donut for your hair in case you want to make a bun." — **Mika**

> "Donuts? Buns? What's all this talk about baked goods?" — **Coco**

> "You wrap your hair around a donut-shaped sponge to make a tight bun. Lulu, if you make it to round #2, which you will, it'd be perfect for the Betsy Ballerina look." — **Kiki**

So far, so good . . . right, Diary? Everyone's having a good time, talking about hair and baked goods. Then:

> "So, Lulu, who are you taking to the red carpet event if you win, Kiki or Coco?" — **Mika**

What, where, who, what now?!

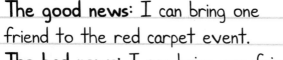

The good news: I can bring one friend to the red carpet event.
The bad news: I can bring one friend to the red carpet event.

"I didn't know that the winner can only bring one friend. How do you know this?" – **me**

"Katy told me, because if she wins, she's taking me." – **Mika**

"Hmmm. Did you know blush can be used as eye shadow?" – **me**

Then Kiki told us one of her fun facts:

In the olden days, when kings and queens arrived somewhere, a red carpet was rolled out to welcome them.

How will I choose who to take to the red carpet event with me if I win? I can't bear to think about it!!! As you might have guessed, Diary, I didn't get much sleep at the Pajama Party last night.

It's time for Cupcake Catch-Up now. Maybe baking will take my mind off this contest.

While the cupcakes were in the oven, Kiki showed me dresses she started designing for the red carpet event if I win the contest.

Later, I overheard Coco asking Mika if she thinks I've made up my mind about taking Kiki to the red carpet event. I HAVEN'T EVEN WON YET!

My cupcakes turned out flat as pancakes. I tried to tell Coco that flat cupcakes — cup-cookies — are the wave of the future! But she was not happy.

I'm too excited about the contest to think about anything else. And who will I take to the red carpet event if I win?????

Sounds like it's list time . . .

COCO VS. KIKI

If I take Coco:

Coco would be happy.

HAPPY COCO

Kiki would be sad.

SAD KIKI

If I take Kiki:

Kiki would be happy.

HAPPY KIKI

Coco would be sad.

SAD COCO

What am I going to do? Maybe I'm better off losing. Well, Diary, I find out tomorrow if I made it to round #2. . . .

Chapter 6

Special Delivery

Sunday

To Do
- wait
- wait
- wait
- wait
- Eat breakfast
- wait

Meow Meow

Meow

Meow

Diary —

Bosco just barked (okay,
she meowed . . .)!

Sometimes that means there's a delivery person on our doorstep. Maybe, possibly, hopefully, from the contest. GULP. Okay, I'm going downstairs. . . . I hope it's good news. . . .

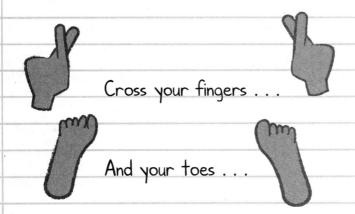

Cross your fingers . . .

And your toes . . .

Okay, so my dad signed for the package. Then he said, "It's from Penelope Glitter Productions! And, Lu, it's a thick one . . . always a good sign . . ."

My dad is really smart.

Penelope Glitter Productions

Lulu Lissette Lyons
8 Lotus Lane
Amber Acres

He knows lots of smart sayings like:

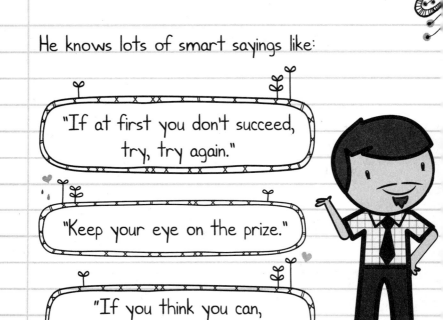

"If at first you don't succeed, try, try again."

"Keep your eye on the prize."

"If you think you can, then you can."

Well, I think I can! And somebody else does, too — LOOK!

iT GiRL MAGAZiNE

Dear Ms. Lyons,

You have been chosen to continue on to the second round of the Sleuth Sally Look-Alike Contest.

Please come to the Amber Acres Mall tomorrow at four p.m. Bring one Sleuth Sally look to model. Please also come prepared to tell us the name of your favorite **charity**. (We will make a donation to the winner's charity.)

Please accept a Sleuth Sally nose and glasses as our gift to you for successfully completing the first round of this three-round contest.

Congratulations!

Best,
Sleuth Sally Look-Alike
Contest Judges

CHARITY =
A group set up to help those in need.

I'm still in the running!!! Oh my goodness! Bosco's so excited she's chasing her tail!!!

And I love these glasses!

This is all REALLY exciting, but I've got work to do. The charity part is easy. I'll talk about All Paws. But what about my next Sleuth Sally look? There are so many to choose from, I don't know how to choose.

"Which Sleuth Sally character should I be?" — me

"Is there a vampire?" — Chantal

"Yes." — me

"Well, duh." — Chantal

Chantal thinks vampires are the answer to everything. Books, TV shows, movies, breakfast cereals. If there's a vampire in it, it <u>has</u> to be good. Let's see if my BFFs agree. . . .

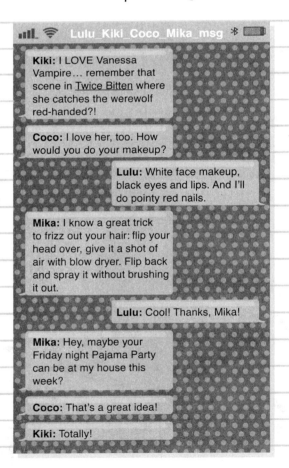

Kiki: I LOVE Vanessa Vampire… remember that scene in <u>Twice Bitten</u> where she catches the werewolf red-handed?!

Coco: I love her, too. How would you do your makeup?

Lulu: White face makeup, black eyes and lips. And I'll do pointy red nails.

Mika: I know a great trick to frizz out your hair: flip your head over, give it a shot of air with blow dryer. Flip back and spray it without brushing it out.

Lulu: Cool! Thanks, Mika!

Mika: Hey, maybe your Friday night Pajama Party can be at my house this week?

Coco: That's a great idea!

Kiki: Totally!

Okay, Vanessa Vampire it is, then!
Mika's hair trick sounds really
cool . . . and that was sweet of
her to offer to host the next
sleepover. I was so wrong about her!

Kiki just called an emergency LLGC meeting. . . .
I wonder what it could be about? Gotta run!

Back from the meeting. My BFFs think we should
add Mika to the LLGC. . . .

LOTUS
LANE

"She does live on Lotus Lane,
right next door to Coco." — Kiki

"And, really, what if she knocked on one
of our doors while we were having an
LLGC club meeting without her? I know I'd
feel bad." — Coco

Everyone was quiet for a moment. Then another moment . . . Then a third moment. Kiki and Coco were waiting for me to say something.

"I guess we can ask Mika to join the LLGC. . . . Then we'll always be able to do things that need to be done in pairs. Like playing tennis, riding roller coasters, and splitting sandwiches." — me

LLGC NOW:

LLGC WITH MIKA:

Coco and Kiki hugged me so hard, I was afraid my eyeballs would pop out. We are going to plan a surprise party for Mika and we'll invite her to join the LLGC at the party! Won't that be fun, Diary?!

I'm glad I know that Mika is a friend. Now I have more time to think about other things, like the fact that round #2 of the contest is TOMORROW!!!!!!!!!!!!

Chapter 7

Biting My Lip

Monday

To Do

- Pack costume
- Pack makeup
- Go to mall right after school (No Super Scrapbooking today so we can all be at the mall)
- Freak out
- Calm down
- Make it to the next round????

When I got to school today, the first thing I saw was Katy Krupski showing Mika a fake nose with glasses. You know what that means? Katy made it to round #2, too!!!! UGH.

Then I saw Katy hand Mika her phone. I guess Mika went to Katy's house last night for dinner or something. I heard Mika say she had left it there by accident. I really hope Katy is nicer to Mika than she is to . . . well . . . everyone else.

Okay, I'm back home from round #2 of the contest, and I take back what I said earlier about hoping Katy is nice to Mika. I don't care what happens to Mika. Do you want to know why? Because when I showed up today, guess who was <u>also</u> dressed as Vanessa Vampire? And guess who <u>also</u> had pointy red nails and frizzed-out hair?!

I'll give you three hints: Katy, Katy, and Katy! And the ONLY people who knew how I'd be dressing up were Coco, Kiki, and MIKA (who was with Katy last night, **BTW**).

BTW = by the way

KATY

OH NO!!!

I CAN'T BELIEVE IT!!

ME

But first, I'll rewind. . . .

Out onstage, the other **contestants** looked amazing. There was a girl dressed like Yodeler Yvonne, who'd clearly been practicing yodeling. She even sang a tune (or yodelled!) for the judges. All vampires do is bite people, and I didn't think the judges would like that.

CONTESTANT = person who competes in a contest

The good news: I made it to round #3!
The bad news: So did Katy Krupski. (The yodeler did, too. Her name is Heidi.)

HEIDI
(THE YODELER)

I guess I shouldn't be surprised that Katy made it to the final round, too. . . . She had a great costume, right down to her pointy red nails.

The judges loved my look and seemed to like hearing about All Paws. I was surprised by how much I cared about the charity part of the contest. When I said how much volunteering at All Paws means to me, I almost cried.

Oh, Diary! I forgot to tell you the best part! You'll never guess what Katy's charity is: Boo-to-Bullying! How can a bully like Katy choose an anti-bullying group as her charity?! She should just stop being a bully!

Anyway, as soon as I stepped offstage, Mom high-fived me. Chantal pulled me in for a hug. "You are <u>this close</u> to your dream!" she said, making the sign for "this close" with her fingers. And my BFFs were right there, too.

"Way to go, Lulu!" – Coco

"You did it!" – Kiki

"I can hardly believe it!" – me

Then I looked over to where Mika was laughing with Katy.

"But can you believe those two?" – me

"Don't even think about Katy!"
                        – Coco and Kiki

On the car ride home, my BFFs showed me the pictures they took.

The pictures looked great, but you could totally see how much Katy and I looked alike.

"I think Mika was a spy, planted by Katy Krupski — a double agent like the one Penelope Glitter plays in the new Sleuth Sally movie." — me

"We don't know anything for sure." — Coco

"Oh, yeah? Then how did Katy's Vanessa Vampire end up looking just like mine?" — me

"Well, that was just a...I mean, it had to be..." — Coco

"At least I didn't have to cheat to make it to the next round!" — me

"Ummm...want some pretzels?" — Kiki

Round #3 - the FINAL round of the contest — is this Thursday. I have to bring three different Sleuth Sally looks and talk more about All Paws. I need to stay focused. Otherwise I might go "cuckoo bananas," as Coco would say.

Chapter 8

Pick One

Tuesday

To Do
- Avoid Mika
- Avoid Katy
- Doggie Day Spa

Something happened at school today that was definitely <u>not</u> on my to-do list. . . .

I passed Mika and Katy in the hallway, and I couldn't exactly avoid them — Mika was waving at me. So I just said a very quiet, very not mean "hi."

But then, before I knew it, I was telling Mika that she had to choose to be friends with me or with Katy. But that she couldn't be friends with both of us. The minute I said it Mika turned red and her eyes got all watery.

"How can I choose when I like both of you?"
— Mika

Then Katy asked me if I was proud of myself. It was awful. . . . All I could do was walk away, feeling like a terrible person. Maybe I made a mistake, Diary?

Thank goodness tonight is Doggie Day Spa. Although this day has been <u>so</u> bad that I kind of wish it was Lulu Day Spa.

During Doggie Day Spa, Coco and Kiki kept getting texts from Mika. She was trying to find out why I'm mad at her.

"Lulu, you told Mika she had to choose between you and Katy?" – Coco

"That's almost like when Sleuth Sally told her boyfriend he had to choose between her and Betsy Ballerina, even though they were the same person!" – Kiki

"It's nothing like that, Kiki." – Coco

"Ladies!" – me

"meow." – Bosco

(Obviously, Bosco was agreeing with me. That or she liked the new doggie nail polish we used tonight: Perfectly Pink.)

By the end of Doggie Day Spa, Coco and Kiki had told Mika I was mad because I thought she had told Katy about my plans for Vanessa Vampire.

Mika: I swear i never told Katy about Vanessa Vampire.

Coco: Then how did she end up wearing the same thing as Lulu, down to the nail tips?

Kiki: Yeah…how?

Mika: I don't know, but I wish Lulu would believe me. I hope you two do.

I don't know what to think, Diary. I'm just glad it's finally time for bed. . . . Night.

Chapter 9

Katy Proof

Wednesday

To Do
- Try new hairdo with braids
- Go to school
- Go to TMM
- Plan 3 looks for round #3!

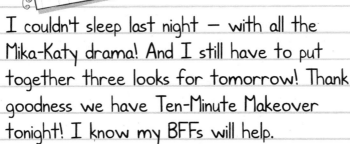

I couldn't sleep last night — with all the Mika-Katy drama! And I still have to put together three looks for tomorrow! Thank goodness we have Ten-Minute Makeover tonight! I know my BFFs will help.

My three Sleuth Sally
looks are going to
be: Betsy Ballerina,
Her Royal Highness Helene,
and Movie Star Mona.
Kiki is bringing **accessories**
to TMM tonight. And Coco's

ACCESSORIES =
outfit
add-ons, like
jewelry, shoes, hats,
and headbands

bringing cupcakes and strawberries! How do people
who don't have a Kiki or a Coco in their lives
survive? Oh, right — I know . . . they have a
Mika nearby to spy for them.

Kiki and Coco are the most amazing friends! Kiki's
accessories look just like the ones Sleuth Sally
wears! And Katy won't be wearing any of these
because they're Kiki Keenan originals!

This beautiful feathered headband is for Betsy
Ballerina:

BETSY
BALLERINA

This jeweled tiara is for
Her Royal Highness Helene:

HER ROYAL
HIGHNESS
HELENE

And these huge sunglasses (that would make
<u>anyone</u> look like a star!) are for Movie Star Mona:

MOVIE STAR
MONA

As we were saying good-bye tonight, Kiki and Coco told me that they don't think Mika said anything to Katy. . . . I know they really like Mika. I was starting to like her, too. But if Mika didn't say anything to Katy, <u>then who did?</u>

DIARY!!! I just climbed into bed to go to sleep, but WAIT!

I totally forgot about Jada! OH NO!!!!!!!!!!!! . . . I said I'd be at All Paws after school tomorrow to see her! And I was going to get there early to give Ada the full Doggie Day Spa treatment so she'd look amazing before Jada meets her!

I'd ask Chantal to go in my place, but she can't go because she's coming to the contest. And my BFFs are coming to the contest, too. But I can't let Jada down!

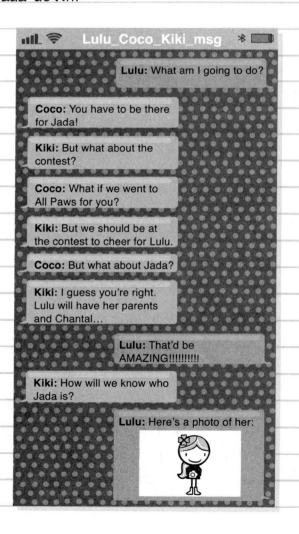

Lulu_Coco_Kiki_msg

Lulu: What am I going to do?

Coco: You have to be there for Jada!

Kiki: But what about the contest?

Coco: What if we went to All Paws for you?

Kiki: But we should be at the contest to cheer for Lulu.

Coco: But what about Jada?

Kiki: I guess you're right. Lulu will have her parents and Chantal…

Lulu: That'd be AMAZING!!!!!!!!!!

Kiki: How will we know who Jada is?

Lulu: Here's a photo of her:

I hope Jada won't be too upset I'm not there tomorrow. But I know that Kiki and Coco will take good care of her, and that they'll give Ada a fabulous makeover. And I can still go to the contest. Phew!

Night, Diary!

Chapter 10

Lu Who?

Thursday

To Do
- Avoid Katy ✓
- Avoid Mika ✓
- Go to mall for round #3!!!
- Win contest??????

EEK X 100

Diary, I'm happy to report that I was able to avoid Katy and Mika all day at school today. Now I'm in the car on the way to the contest. I can't even write because I'm too nervous to hold my pen. Wish me luck!

It's all over, Diary. I'll tell you about it from the beginning. . . .

As soon as I got to the mall, I knew it was going to be hard to win the contest. Heidi and Katy both looked great.

"Stop worrying about the other contestants. You're <u>thisclose</u> to your dream!" – **Chantal**

Then Kiki sent me a picture of her and Coco with Jada and Ada.

Jada looked so happy that I really didn't care about anything else. Yay!

Then it was time to get started. The judges
explained that we could lose at any time — today,
each part (the three looks plus the charity speech)
was like its own mini-contest. I was so nervous!!!

My first costume (Her Royal Highness Helene)
looked FABULOUS! Next came Heidi. She looked
amazing as Fortune-Teller Francine. She had lots
of bracelets and big hoop earrings. I started
to worry. Then came Katy . . . also dressed as
Fortune-Teller Francine! Did she somehow spy on
Heidi, too?

The worst part was that Katy's costume looked better than Heidi's. She had a magic crystal ball and kept saying, "I see Penelope Glitter in my future." The judges really liked that.

Heidi →

So poor Heidi lost,
and Katy and I tied.
Then we tied the next two looks, too!!
Here's a rundown of how we did in each round:

ROUND:	ME:	KATY:	WINNER:
#1	Her Royal Highness Helene	Fortune-Teller Francine	Tie
#2	Betsy Ballerina	Circus Clown Coleen	Tie!
#3	Movie Star Mona	Cat Burglar Clarissa	Tie!!

And here are all of our Sleuth Sally looks:

Me

Katy

Her Royal Highness Helene

Fortune-Teller Francine

Betsy Ballerina

Circus Clown Coleen

Movie Star Mona

Cat Burglar Clarissa

Next I had to talk about the best part of working at All Paws. I took a deep breath. Then I said, "The best part is seeing how good the pets can make people feel." I spoke about Jada and about how sad she was when she came in last week. Then I pulled out my phone to show the judges how happy she looks now that she has Ada. . . .

As I scrolled through my messages for the picture my BFFs had just sent, I saw my texts from last week about my vampire costume.

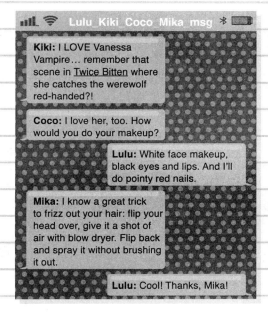

Kiki: I LOVE Vanessa Vampire… remember that scene in <u>Twice Bitten</u> where she catches the werewolf red-handed?!

Coco: I love her, too. How would you do your makeup?

Lulu: White face makeup, black eyes and lips. And I'll do pointy red nails.

Mika: I know a great trick to frizz out your hair: flip your head over, give it a shot of air with blow dryer. Flip back and spray it without brushing it out.

Lulu: Cool! Thanks, Mika!

That's how Katy knew! Mika forgot her phone at Katy's house! Then Katy looked at Mika's texts and saw the one from me about my costume! Mika wasn't to blame after all!!

One of the judges cleared her throat. Oops! Before I had more time to think, I showed the photo of Jada and Ada. They all smiled.

Just then, a new text came in:

Kiki_Lulu_msg

Kiki: We're here!

Sure enough, I looked out and saw Kiki and Coco in the audience with Jada and Ada! I told the judges they were the ones from the photo. (Jada's mom had brought everyone to watch the contest. How great is that?!)

Then Katy came out onstage to talk about her charity, the Boo-to-Bullying Group. She talked about how important the group was to her as a former bully. CAN YOU BELIEVE HER?! She is definitely <u>still</u> a bully! She did sound believable, though. She even shed a tear! One perfect crystal-shaped tear.

The judges huddled together for a few minutes. Then the main judge said:

"Ladies and gentlemen, this was a difficult decision but we have finally chosen a winner. And the winner of the Sleuth Sally Look-Alike Contest is Katy Krupski. . . ."

I was trying as hard as I possibly could to hold back tears and even to smile. I started to head offstage when I thought I heard the judge say the word "And."

And? And what?

Forty-five hours later,
I heard "Lu."

Lu? Lu who?

It was a tie! Katy and I both won the contest! And we will both meet Penelope Glitter TOMORROW!!!

But . . . I still didn't know who I should take with me to the movie premiere. This was the BEST part, Diary. The judges said Coco, Kiki, and Jada could _all_ come with me! I didn't have to choose between them after all!!! I guess the judges were wowed by how helpful they all were.

What an amazing day! I'm not sure how I'll ever get to sleep tonight! I'm going to meet Penelope Glitter TOMORROW!!!!!!!

(BTW, it sure looks like I owe Mika a BIG apology tomorrow, doesn't it?)

penelope glitter

Chapter 11

Lights, Camera, Action!

Friday

☆To Do☆

- Go to school
- Get ready
- Go to movie premiere
- Meet Penelope Glitter!!!
- Have Pajama Party at Mika's house!

Oh my, Diary — did you see my to-do list for today? It's the best to-do list EVER!

Kiki: I'm too excited to go to school!

Lulu: I was just thinking the same thing!

Coco: How can we sit still when we're going to meet Penelope Glitter tonight?!

Well, off to the looooooooongest eight hours of my life.

We all just finished getting dressed up to go to the premiere. My LLGC girls were here and Jada, too. (Mika's getting ready over at Katy's house so we're just going to see her at the premiere.) Look, Diary, here are some photos my dad took of us getting ready. . . .

Pretty glamorous, right?

Diary, walking on the red carpet was AMAZING! It was exactly like all the red carpet events I've seen on TV! Except instead of being at home with my sweats on, I was at the event, wearing a gown and feeling oh-so-glamorous.

As I walked along, I felt like a real famous person, or even a princess. I was a little nervous when we first met Penelope. She's even cooler in real life than she is in the movies.

Here's a picture of the six of us with Penelope:

The movie, *Double Trouble*, was amazing, too. Penelope played Sleuth Sally playing a pair of twins. She said sometimes it got very confusing, but that it was the most fun Sleuth Sally movie to make. It was the most fun Sleuth Sally movie to watch as well!

At the **after party** 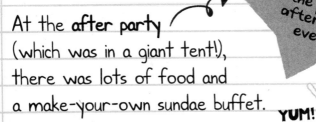 (which was in a giant tent!), there was lots of food and a make-your-own sundae buffet.

AFTER PARTY = the party after a big event

YUM!

When it was time to go, Jada took me aside to thank me for everything. I told her I couldn't have helped her without my friends' help. I also said I hoped she'd hang out with us again soon. Then we hugged. She's so sweet!!

After Jada's mom took her home, I walked over to where Coco and Kiki were standing. I told them what I figured out about Mika's phone. They gave me a <u>look</u>. We all knew it was time for me to apologize to Mika. We're (right now!) piled into Mika's mom's car heading to the sleepover. I'll have to update you in the morning, Diary! More to come . . .

Chapter 12

It Girls!

Saturday

To Do
- wake up
- Get copy of <u>It Girl!</u>
- Go crazy!!!

It's hard to get out of bed on the day after the **BEST NIGHT OF YOUR LIFE!**

To update you, Diary, I apologized to Mika for being mad at her and for asking her to choose between me and Katy. Mika was surprised when I told her what I think happened with Katy and with her phone. She said she'd talk to Katy about it. She seemed pretty upset. I'm not sure if they'll work it out or not, but I'm thankful that I can trust Mika to be a good friend to me. She was behind me 100% throughout this contest, and I shouldn't have doubted her friendship for one second. She can be friends with whoever else she wants!

I can't wait till we surprise Mika by asking her to join the LLGC next week! Kiki and Coco are already planning the <u>surprise</u> party!!

SHHH! SHHH!

Okay, the new issue of *It Girl!* comes out today. I'm going to go get it now!

I just saw my picture in *It Girl!* — I'm famous! (Sort of . .) I'm too excited to write. Excuse me while I go run around the block a few hundred times and shout for joy, loud enough for the whole world to hear. The LLGC met PENELOPE GLITTER!!!!!

I'll be back as soon as I calm down . . . um . . . I'm not sure when that will be! Don't wait up!

Xoxo,
Lulu

Kyla May

lives near the beach in Australia with her husband, three daughters, two dogs, two cats, and four guinea pigs.

As a child, Kyla spent many hours dressing up as famous people — often as Olivia Newton-John, Madonna, or Marilyn Monroe. As seen in this photo, Kyla would lick red candy and wipe the coloring onto her lips, pretending it was lipstick. These days, Kyla's three young daughters often play dress-up. Sometimes Kyla helps with their hairdos, and on special occasions, she even lets them wear makeup!

Kyla's first passion is drawing. Her second is chocolate.

Look at the lists on page 11. How are Penelope and Lulu **similar**?

Why doesn't Lulu like Katy Krupski?

How does Lulu's opinion of Mika **change** throughout the book? How does Mika's opinion of Katy **change** throughout the book?

Create your own charity! Give your charity a name. Write down **who** it will help, **what** the volunteers will do, and **why** it is important to you.

Do you think the Lotus Lane girls should invite Mika to join their club? Use examples from the book to make your argument.